About the Author

Austin Haigh was born in Chesterfield, in 1975, and currently resides in Bakewell, Derbyshire with his wife Sophie and 2 children. Scarlett and the Gingerbread House is his first published material, although he is always surrounded by books, managing at a major high street book chain (The Works) for well over a decade.

Scarlett and the Gingerbread House

Austin Haigh

Scarlett and the Gingerbread House

Olympia Publishers
London

www.olympiapublishers.com
OLYMPIA PAPERBACK EDITION

A CIP catalogue record for this title is available from the British Library.

ISBN: 978-1-78830-815-1
First Published in 2020

Olympia Publishers
Tallis House
2 Tallis Street
London
EC4Y 0AB

Printed in Great Britain

Dedication

This book is dedicated to my Nan, Mary Pursglove.
Who always taught me that anything is possible.

Acknowledgements

I'd like to acknowledge my wife Sophie and all of our beautiful family, but of course, especially our daughter Scarlett. She is obviously the inspiration for this one. This story is for you Scarlett.

This is the story of Scarlett. She lives with her mummy and daddy, in a house that was made completely out of gingerbread. One morning Scarlett woke up, got out of bed, ate her breakfast and got ready for school. She said goodbye to her mummy and daddy and her mummy and daddy both said, "Goodbye Scarlett, have a good day at school... and don't eat any gingerbread!"

As Scarlett went out of the front of her gingerbread house, she closed the door behind her, but the handle just came off in her hand.

So Scarlett took the gingerbread door handle onto the school bus with her. She found an empty seat, sat down and ate it.

When she arrived at school, she learned all sorts of new and exciting things, but her teachers were very cross with her because she didn't eat her dinner.

After Scarlett had finished school, she returned home on the school bus. She ran straight back into her gingerbread house, and then she called out "Mummy, Daddy, the gingerbread door handle came off in my hand this morning and I ate it."'

Mummy and Daddy both said "Oh Scarlett, we told you not to eat our house... but never mind, just don't eat anymore!"

Scarlett agreed that she wouldn't and then she went into her gingerbread bedroom. She went to close her bedroom window, which was slightly ajar, and it fell off into her hand. She took one look at it and then she gobbled it all up.

After a goodnight's sleep, Scarlett opened her eyes. Her bedroom was just full of animals.

There was a barn owl, a rabbit, a chimpanzee and two foxes. They had all climbed in through the open space where her window once was.

She got up, cleaned her teeth and got dressed, but she didn't eat her breakfast though because her tummy was still full from all the gingerbread that she had eaten the previous night. As she went out of the front door, she gave her mummy and daddy a kiss goodbye and they both said, "Goodbye Scarlett, we love you very much... and don't eat any more gingerbread!"

Scarlett closed the front door behind her, and can you guess what happened? The whole entire door came off it's gingerbread hinges. So she picked it up and carried it onto the school bus with her.

She sat at the very back of the bus that morning and shared all of her gingerbread with all of the other children on the bus. And that day the teachers were very, very cross, because none of the children on the school bus that day ate any of their dinners.

When Scarlett got home that day, she told her mummy and daddy all about her day, and her mummy and daddy both said, "Scarlett we are very pleased that you had a good day and practiced how to share, but please, please, please stop eating our home!"

Scarlett ate up her tea, did her homework, and retreated into her gingerbread bedroom. As she closed the door behind her, it only fell right off its gingerbread hinges... so she fed it to all the animals (who were still all there). The owl, the rabbit, the chimpanzee and both of the foxes - all shared a gingerbread supper.

The very next day, Scarlett woke up (as usual), went downstairs (as usual), and ate her breakfast. She had cornflakes and she told her mummy and daddy all about the animals in her bedroom. She got dressed into her school uniform and as she went out of the front of the house, can you just guess what happened?

The whole entire front wall of the house collapsed onto the floor. Now it was massive, so she couldn't possibly fit it onto the school bus, could she? So that morning she walked into school carrying it over her head.

When she got to school on this occasion, at first the teachers were very angry. But then Scarlett explained that she had bought it in for all the teachers to share and that made them happy... although that day none of the teachers ate their dinner.

After a very interesting day at school, where Scarlett had learned all about the lifecycle of nature, and other things. She returned home to her gingerbread house. Although, I say gingerbread house, it was more like 3 gingerbread walls now with a roof on top to keep them dry.

Scarlett told her Mummy and Daddy all about her day and then she went into her gingerbread bedroom. She fed the animals with a gingerbread wall then it was time for Scarlett's tea. For their tea her family shared the rest of the house.

Mummy and Daddy each had a gingerbread wall and Scarlett had the gingerbread roof.

That night they slept in a tent!

The next morning Mummy was up bright and early, and she was cooking something in the oven. When Scarlett awoke, she started to cry. "Daddy," she said, "we've eaten our beautiful house all up and now we have nowhere to live!"

Daddy said, "Don't worry Scarlett, Mummy is baking us a brand new house right now, it will be ready for when you get home from school today!"

All day Scarlett was so excited she just couldn't wait to finish school. When she got home that afternoon there was indeed a brand-new gingerbread house waiting. It was bigger and better than the last one and it even had a chocolate fountain outside.

Mummy and Daddy were also very pleased with their new gingerbread house. "But Scarlett," they both said together, "this is our new house! It's big and it's beautiful, but it is completely made out of gingerbread. So please, please, please, whatever you do... don't eat any of the gingerbread!"